A Very Long Time

written by

Geri Timperley and Nikki Arro

illustrated by

Marlaina Kopietz

Beaver's Pond Press, Inc.
Edina · Minnesota

ISBN 1-59298-119-4

Library of Congress Catalog Number: 2005929437

Printed in the United States of America

First Printing: August 2005

09 08 07 06 05   6 5 4 3 2 1

Cover and interior design by Rachel Holscher
Typesetting by Stanton Publication Services, Inc.

Beaver's Pond Press, Inc.

7104 Ohms Lane, Suite 216
Edina, MN 55439-2129
(952) 829-8818
www.BeaversPondPress.com

To order, visit www.BookHouseFulfillment.com or call
1-800-901-3480. Reseller discounts available.

To all the men and women who are so
bravely serving our country and to the families that
support them and wait A VERY LONG TIME
for their safe return.

One day at daycare a boy said to me,

"You don't have a dad!"

"Yes, I do," I said.

"Well, he never picks you up," he said.

I looked at him and said in my most grown-up voice,

"My daddy's at drill for . . ."

I know about a very long time.

My mommy talks to me about it a lot.

Like when my mommy was waiting for

my daddy to ask her to marry him.

Mommy had to wait . . .

. . . a very long time.

Then, when my mommy found out that

she was going to have a baby,

she and my daddy had to wait for me to be born,

and they said it felt like . . .

And when I ask my mommy,
"When is it going to be Christmas
or my birthday again?",
she always says, "In a little while."
'A little while' always takes . . .

. . . a very long time.

One day my daddy put me in his lap and

told me that he was going to help some people

and protect our country very far away.

My daddy said he was going to be gone for . . .

. . . a very long time.

On the morning my daddy left for his very long drill,

my mommy and I got up very early. We took Daddy

to a very big bus with all kinds of other daddies and

mommies and kids too. When it was time to say goodbye,

I hugged my daddy and said, "I will miss you for . . ."

"... a very long time."

When my daddy was gone I got very lonely.

Grandma helped me make a paper chain with the number

of weeks until my daddy would be home. We made . . .

. . . a very long chain.

Auntie Nikki had her students write letters

and draw pictures and bring treats for my daddy.

I helped her pack it all up. It went in a very big box.

Now my daddy would have enough

letters and treats to last . . .

. . . a very long time.

Sometimes I got very sad and wished my
daddy was home. My mommy told me my daddy
was helping make the world a safer and better place.
She said lots of people in America and even the President
would be very proud of my daddy for . . .

Mommy said that we needed to be brave like Daddy.

I made my daddy a picture and I told Mommy to

write on it, "I am brave like you, Daddy!"

I kept asking, "Daddy, did you get my picture yet?"

He said the mail takes . . .

. . . a very long time.

I waited and waited and counted the days

on a calendar until my daddy would come home.

It would be two birthdays and one Christmas.

That means I had to wait . . .

Finally, Mommy said that we were going to

the airport to pick up Daddy. I asked the whole way,

"Are we there yet, Mommy?" She said,

"Not yet!", even though we had been

riding in the car for . . .

When all the people were getting off the plane
I watched and waited for my daddy. I saw him walking
way down the ramp. I ran as fast as I could and jumped
into his arms. My daddy hugged me and kissed me
and cried with me for . . .

The next day Daddy brought me to daycare.

I tell everyone that my daddy has come home.

I am so happy that my daddy is home.

Now he will be mine FOREVER, and that is . . .

The End.